For Brian and Daphne

First published 1988 by Walker Books Ltd

87 Vauxhall Walk, London SE11 5HJ

This edition published 2006

8 10 9 7

© 1988 and 2005 Penny Dale

The right of Penny Dale to be identified as author/illustrator of this work
has been asserted by her in accordance with the Copyright, Designs and Patents Act 1988

This book has been typset in StempelSchneidler

Printed in China

British Library Cataloguing in Publication Data: a catalogue record for this book is
available from the British Library

ISBN 978-1-4063-0035-2

www.walker.co.uk

TEN IN THE BED

PENNY DALE

WALKER BOOKS
AND SUBSIDIARIES

LONDON • BOSTON • SYDNEY • AUCKLAND

There were ten in the bed and the little one said,
"Roll over, roll over!"

So they all rolled over and Hedgehog fell out ... BUMP!

There were nine in the bed and the little one said,
"Roll over, roll over!"
So they all rolled over and Zebra fell out ... OUCH!

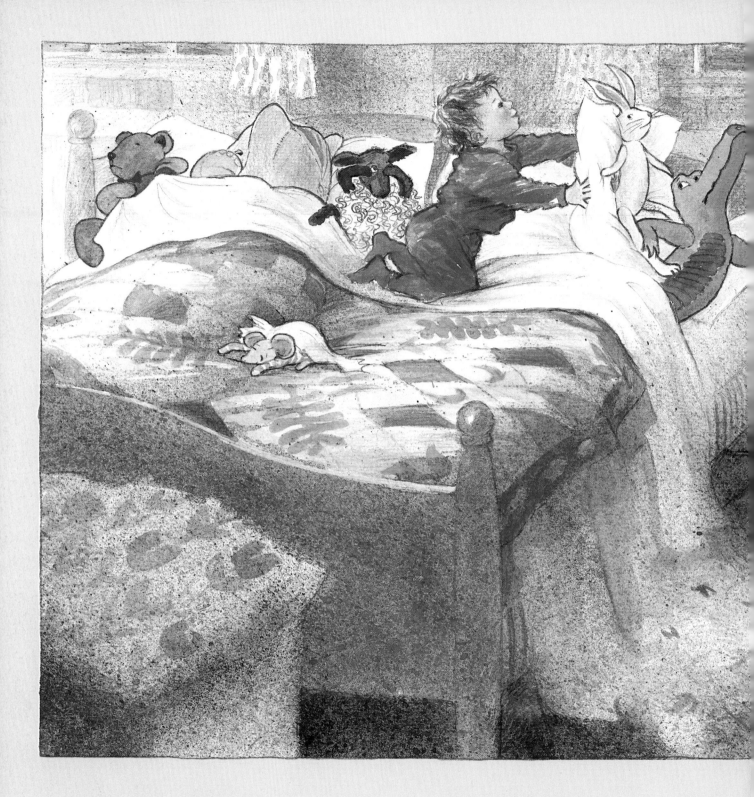

There were eight in the bed and the little one said,
"Roll over, roll over!"
So they all rolled over and Ted fell out ... THUMP!

There were seven in the bed and the little one said,
"Roll over, roll over!"
So they all rolled over and Croc fell out ... THUD!

There were six in the bed and the little one said,
"Roll over, roll over!"
So they all rolled over and Rabbit fell out ... BONK!

There were five in the bed and the little one said,

"Roll over, roll over!"

So they all rolled over and Mouse fell out ... DINK!

There were four in the bed and the little one said,
"Roll over, roll over!"
So they all rolled over and Nellie fell out … CRASH!

There were three in the bed and the little one said,
"Roll over, roll over!"
So they all rolled over and Bear fell out ... SLAM!

There were two in the bed and the little one said,
"Roll over, roll over!"
So they all rolled over and Sheep fell out ... DONK!

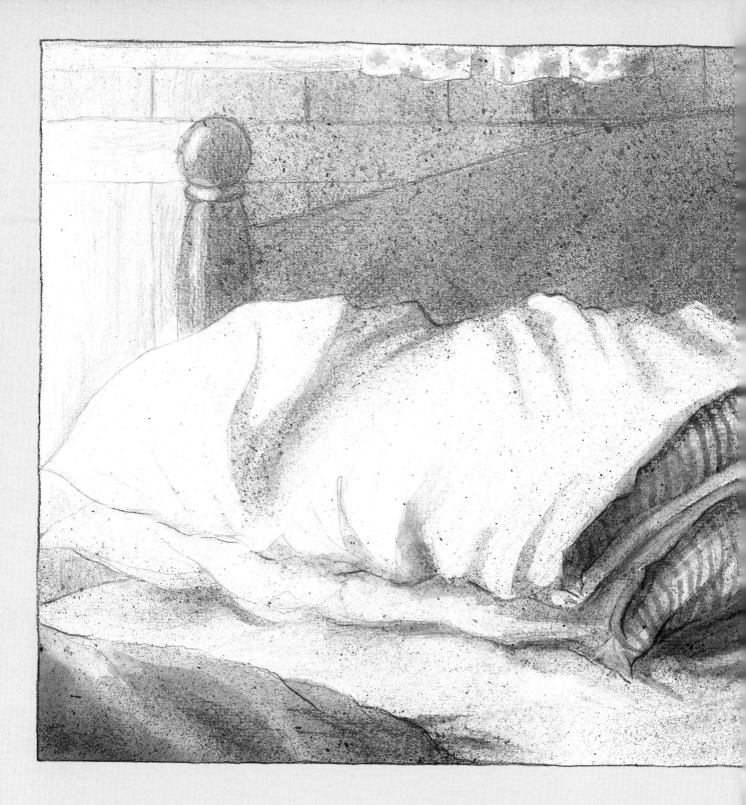

There was one in the bed and the little one said,

"I'm cold! I miss you!"

So they all came back ...

and jumped into bed – Hedgehog, Mouse,
Nellie, Zebra, Ted,

the little one, Rabbit,
Croc, Bear and Sheep.

Ten in the bed, all fast asleep.

The End